SNIPP, SNAPP, SNURR, AND
THE BUTTERED BREAD

By Maj Lindman

ALBERT WHITMAN & COMPANY
CHICAGO   ILLINOIS

19 46

THE FLICKA, RICKA, DICKA BOOKS

By Maj Lindman

FLICKA, RICKA, DICKA, AND THE STRAWBERRIES
FLICKA, RICKA, DICKA, AND THEIR NEW FRIEND
FLICKA, RICKA, DICKA, AND THE NEW DOTTED DRESSES
FLICKA, RICKA, DICKA, AND THE GIRL NEXT DOOR
FLICKA, RICKA, DICKA, AND THE THREE KITTENS

THE SNIPP, SNAPP, SNURR BOOKS

By Maj Lindman

SNIPP, SNAPP, SNURR AND THE RED SHOES
SNIPP, SNAPP, SNURR AND THE GINGERBREAD
SNIPP, SNAPP, SNURR AND THE MAGIC HORSE
SNIPP, SNAPP, SNURR AND THE BUTTERED BREAD
SNIPP, SNAPP, SNURR AND THE YELLOW SLED
SNIPP, SNAPP, SNURR AND THE BIG SURPRISE

FOREWORD

THIS is the fourth book in the series telling of the adventures of Snipp, Snapp, and Snurr. By this time these three little Swedish boys have become firmly entrenched in the affections of American children. Now Snipp, Snapp, and Snurr appear in overalls and go to the farm in quest of milk.

The story has the same quaint charm as the preceding ones. It has an air of reality but it takes just a step over the border of fancy. It is a pleasant book to read when children have had the experience of making butter, just as SNIPP, SNAPP, SNURR, AND THE GINGERBREAD enhances the experience of making gingerbread cookies.

The books are entirely independent of each other. They may be read in any order, and children who first meet Snipp, Snapp, and Snurr at the farm can then go back and read any of the three other adventures.

Alice Dalgliesh

Columbia University
New York City

"You may have a slice of bread without butter," Mother said.

SNIPP, SNAPP, AND SNURR, the little Swedish boys, came running in to their mother in the kitchen.

"Oh, Mummy," they cried, "we are so hungry! We want some bread and butter."

Mother brought a big round loaf of bread out of the cupboard.

"There is no butter left," she said. "But if you are hungry you may have a slice of bread without butter. After that, take the milk can and go to Aunt Annie's. Ask her if you may buy some milk so that I may cream it and make butter. Then tomorrow there will be butter for your bread."

THE boys decided that this was a very good idea.

So they took the milk can and set off for the little red cottage where Aunt Annie and Uncle Freddie lived.

"Aunt Annie," said Snipp, Snapp, and Snurr, "please let us have some milk. Mother wants to cream it and make butter for our bread."

"Dear me," said Aunt Annie, "I have no milk. Blossom will not give me any. But go to the cow shed and ask her gently. Perhaps she will give YOU some milk."

"Please let us have some milk, Aunt Annie."

SO the three little boys went to the cow shed. They saw at once that something was wrong. Blossom stood in her stall munching her dry hay and looking very sad and unhappy.

"Oh, Blossom dear," said Snipp, and stroked her softly on her back, "will you please give us some milk?"

"With plenty of cream," said Snapp.

"So that mother can make butter," added Snurr.

Blossom shook her head and looked sadder than ever.

"I know what she needs," said Snipp. "Fresh green grass. Let's go to Uncle Freddie and tell him so."

"O Blossom, dear, will you please give us some milk?"

THE boys went out of the cow shed. In the meadow they found Uncle Freddie, who was Blossom's master. He looked really downhearted.

"Uncle Freddie," Snipp began, "do give Blossom some green grass, please."

"So that we may buy some milk," Snapp went on.

"So that mother can make butter for our bread," added Snurr.

But Blossom's master looked very sad. He pointed out over the meadow.

"Look around," he said, "see how dark and cold the earth is. No grass can grow without the sun. It is a long time since we have had any sunshine. Ask the sun to start shining. Then perhaps you may soon have butter on your bread."

"Uncle Freddie, do give Blossom some green grass."

WELL, what was to be done? Ask the sun! How could three little boys reach the sun when he was so far away?

They sat down by the roadside to think over the matter.

"We could not possibly ask the sun," said Snipp.

"No," said Snapp, "but what shall we do?"

"Perhaps we could eat our bread without butter," suggested Snurr. "That will do, too."

But the sun, who was hiding behind the clouds, suddenly peeped out at the little boys. He seemed curious to know which little boy was speaking so sensibly.

"But what shall we do?"

WHEN the sun saw the three little brothers with their red cheeks and bright eyes, he came all the way out from behind the clouds and smiled his sunniest smile.

And when the boys saw his shining face they jumped to their feet and began dancing with joy.

"Hoo-ray!" they cried at the top of their voices. "Now Blossom will have her grass, and we will buy milk and mother will make butter for our bread. Hoo-ray!"

The sun looked down at the boys and shone and gleamed and beamed with happiness. So after that there was no end of sunshine.

The sun smiled his sunniest smile.

IT was not long before the grass began to grow. Snipp, Snapp, and Snurr watched it change from day to day until it became green and juicy.

Blossom's master brought his scythe. The grass fell in broad ribbons and the air was fragrant with the scent of clover blossoms and new-mown grass.

Aunt Annie brought a big basket and the three boys helped her to fill it with fresh grass.

Then they all carried the basket to the cow shed where poor Blossom stood, longing for some fresh food. Very soon her manger was filled with the new-mown grass. Oh, how glad she was.

They all carried the basket to the cow shed.

AUNT ANNIE brought her milk pail and sat down on the little low three-legged stool. She leaned her head against Blossom's soft skin and began milking.

The warm milk ran down, fine and white, into the pail. Blossom chewed comfortably and flapped her ears to show everyone how happy she was.

Snipp, Snapp, and Snurr, who had scrambled on to the fence, waited patiently for the milk pail to be full. Then Aunt Annie filled their milk can to the brim with the foaming milk and the little boys went home to their mother with their burden.

Aunt Annie leaned her head against Blossom's soft skin.

THE next morning Mother creamed the milk and poured the cream into the churn. While she worked with the dasher, up and down, up and down without stopping, the boys watched her eagerly.

When the yellow butter was ready and lay salted and molded in the trough, Mother cut three slices from the big round loaf of bread and spread the butter on them.

So Snipp and Snapp and Snurr got their bread and butter at last, and oh, how good it tasted.

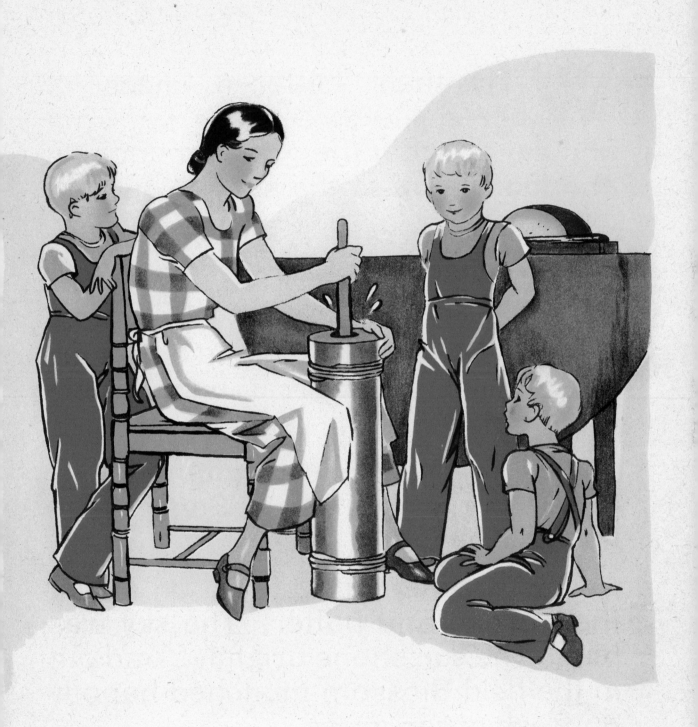

The boys watched her eagerly.

WITH their buttered slices of bread the three boys went out and sat down in the grass, munching and looking up at the sun.

"Now the grass is growing taller and greener every day," said Snipp between two bites of bread and butter.

"And Blossom eats and gives us more milk," said Snapp, taking a big mouthful.

"And we shall have butter on our bread every day," said Snurr, also taking a bite.

The three little boys went on eating their bread and butter. The sky was blue. The sun shone brightly. And out in the field Blossom munched happily on fresh green grass.

The three boys went out and sat down in the grass.